Pipiolo
and the
Roof Dogs

FOR
Marina and Lela
AND
Rebeca and Lupe
AND
in loving memory of Nebaj
—B.A.M. *&* P.E.

Text copyright © 2003 by Brian Meunier
Illustrations copyright © 2003 by Perky Edgerton

CIP Data is available.

Published in the United States by Dutton Children's Books,
a division of Penguin Young Readers Group
345 Hudson Street, New York, New York 10014
www.penguinputnam.com

Designed by Heather Wood
Manufactured in China / First Edition
ISBN 0-525-47128-6
10 9 8 7 6 5 4 3 2 1

BRIAN MEUNIER

Pipiolo and the Roof Dogs

PAINTINGS BY
PERKY EDGERTON

Dutton Children's Books / New York

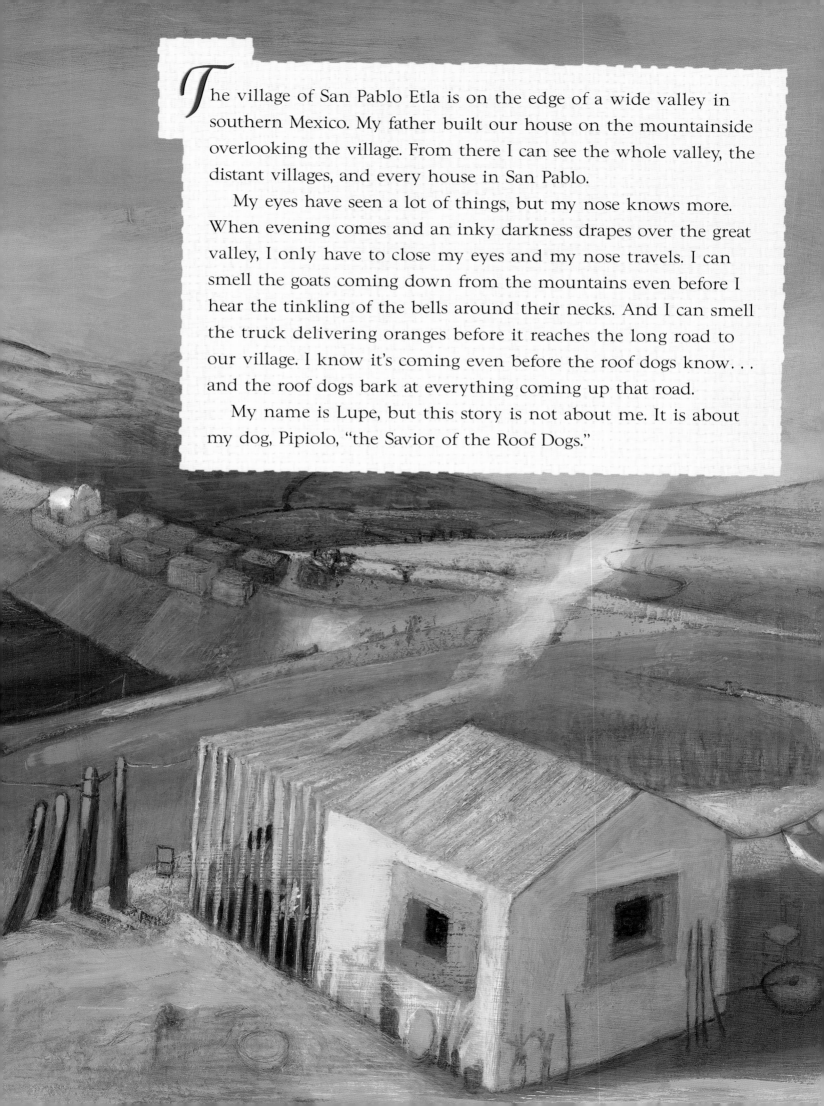

The village of San Pablo Etla is on the edge of a wide valley in southern Mexico. My father built our house on the mountainside overlooking the village. From there I can see the whole valley, the distant villages, and every house in San Pablo.

My eyes have seen a lot of things, but my nose knows more. When evening comes and an inky darkness drapes over the great valley, I only have to close my eyes and my nose travels. I can smell the goats coming down from the mountains even before I hear the tinkling of the bells around their necks. And I can smell the truck delivering oranges before it reaches the long road to our village. I know it's coming even before the roof dogs know. . . and the roof dogs bark at everything coming up that road.

My name is Lupe, but this story is not about me. It is about my dog, Pipiolo, "the Savior of the Roof Dogs."

I found Pipiolo five years ago, near a path on the edge of our cornfield. He was curled up asleep inside an old shoe, and he must have been only a few weeks old. As I bent down to take a closer look, he raised his tiny head and looked me straight in the eye. And I saw greatness.

Pipiolo was such a perky puppy! So anxious to start the day that he would wake me even before the rooster crowed. We would spend our days sniffing in the mountains, exploring all the wonderful aromas the world had to offer.

At night Pipiolo slept outside, under my window. Through the cracks of our adobe house, I could smell him sleeping.

I could smell his dreams.

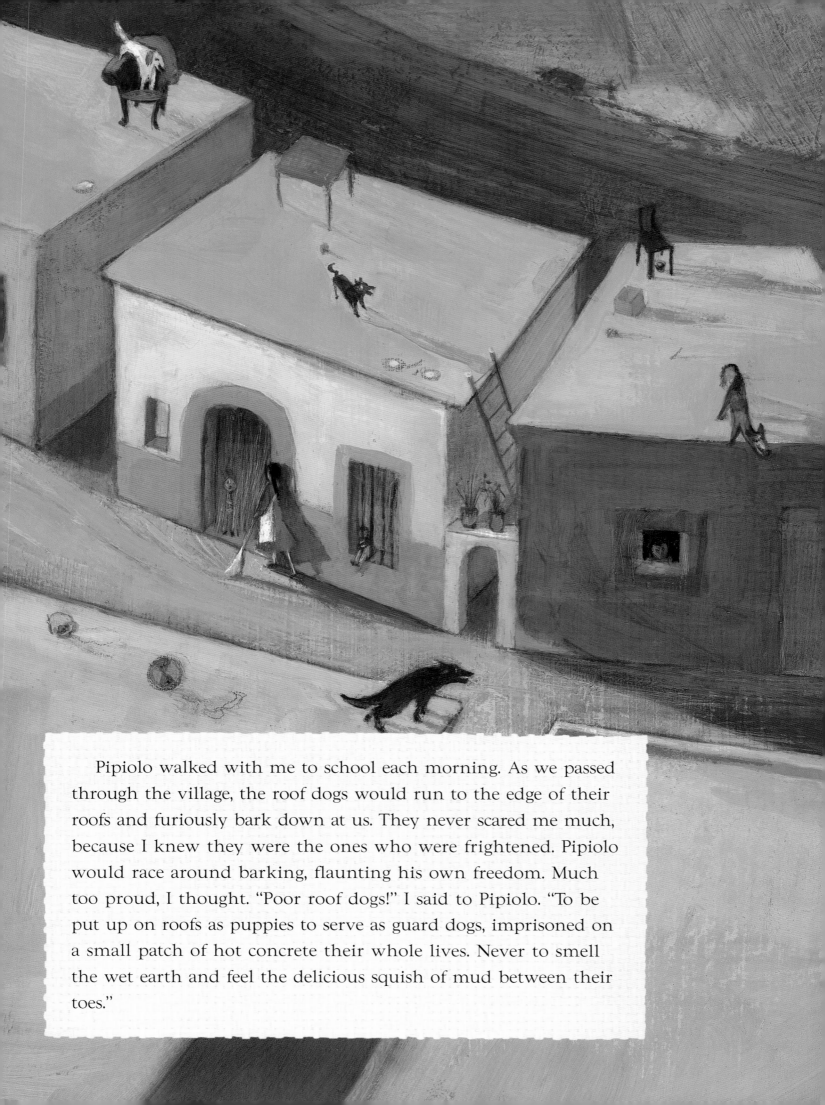

Pipiolo walked with me to school each morning. As we passed through the village, the roof dogs would run to the edge of their roofs and furiously bark down at us. They never scared me much, because I knew they were the ones who were frightened. Pipiolo would race around barking, flaunting his own freedom. Much too proud, I thought. "Poor roof dogs!" I said to Pipiolo. "To be put up on roofs as puppies to serve as guard dogs, imprisoned on a small patch of hot concrete their whole lives. Never to smell the wet earth and feel the delicious squish of mud between their toes."

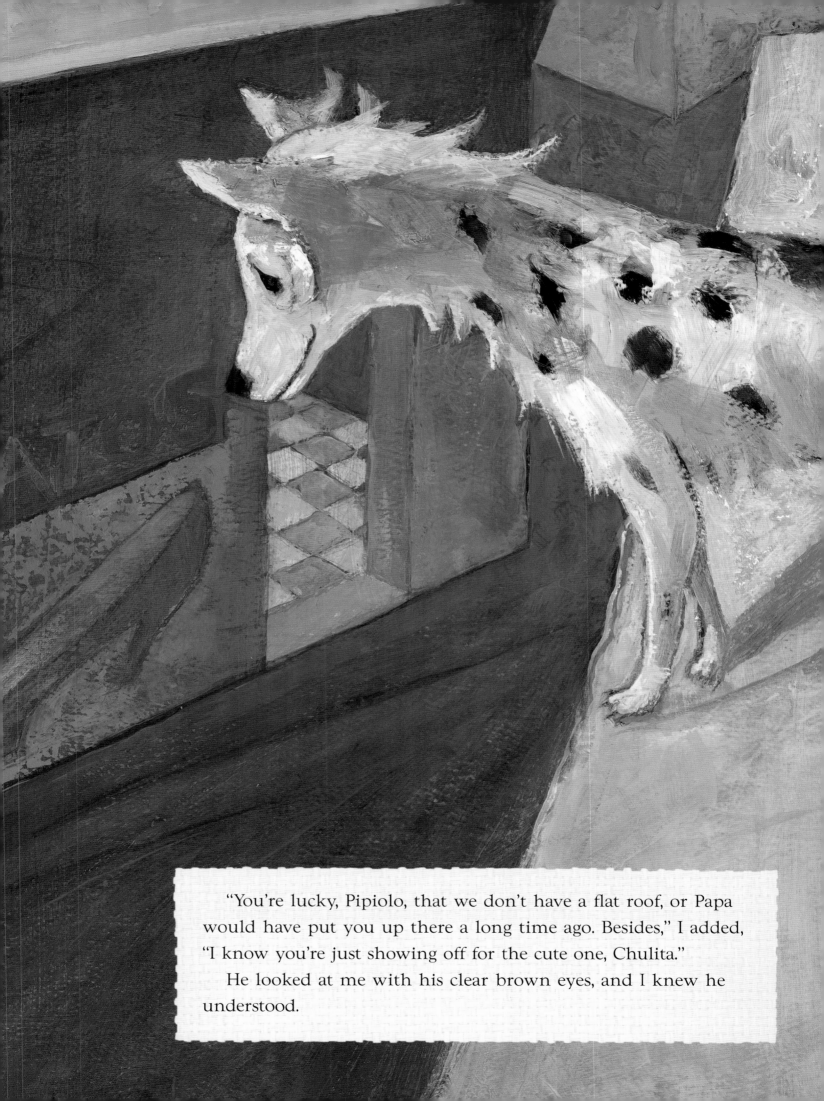

"You're lucky, Pipiolo, that we don't have a flat roof, or Papa would have put you up there a long time ago. Besides," I added, "I know you're just showing off for the cute one, Chulita."

He looked at me with his clear brown eyes, and I knew he understood.

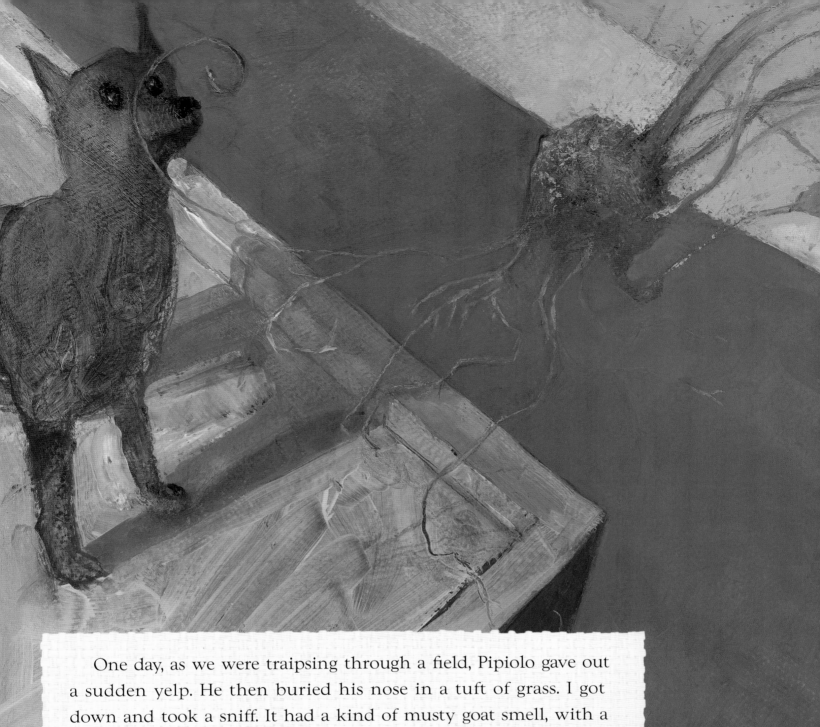

One day, as we were traipsing through a field, Pipiolo gave out a sudden yelp. He then buried his nose in a tuft of grass. I got down and took a sniff. It had a kind of musty goat smell, with a hint of mint. Suddenly, I understood what Pipiolo was trying to tell me!

Using my school ruler as a shovel, I dug up a clump and stuffed it into my backpack. We ran to the village, where I broke the clump into many pieces. I tossed a piece to each angry roof dog, saving the piece with the flower in it for Chulita.

You should have heard the dogs as they experienced their first whiff of real earth—their barks turned from anger to delight. A unified howl of surprise and discovery! And Pipiolo and I howled right along with them in their symphony of celebration.

We had made a difference!

Every day, Pipiolo and I would dig up another fragrance and share it with the roof dogs. We worked hard to find a good variety, sometimes overlooking the very pungent for the rare and unusual.

Life went on like this for some time, until it dawned on me that, on many days, Pipiolo would not even get up with me in the morning to walk to school. He was spending more and more time sleeping in the shade during the day, while I was doing all the work myself in the hot sun!

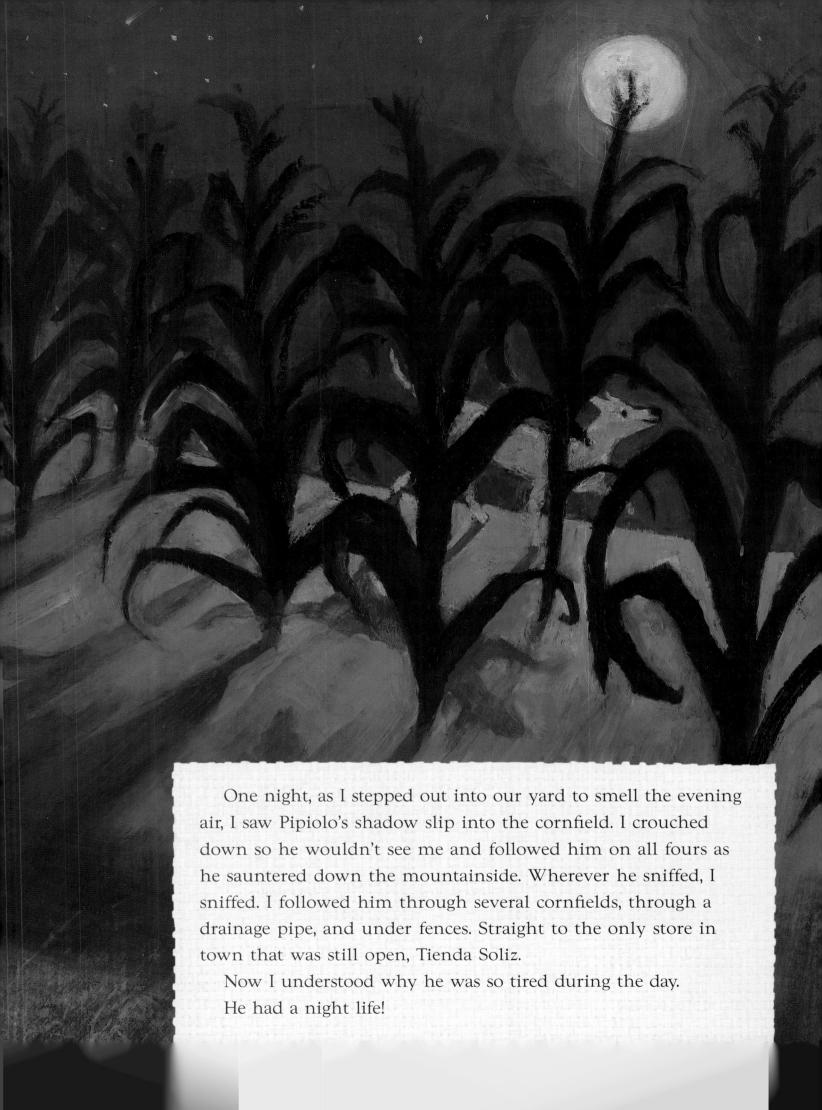

One night, as I stepped out into our yard to smell the evening air, I saw Pipiolo's shadow slip into the cornfield. I crouched down so he wouldn't see me and followed him on all fours as he sauntered down the mountainside. Wherever he sniffed, I sniffed. I followed him through several cornfields, through a drainage pipe, and under fences. Straight to the only store in town that was still open, Tienda Soliz.

Now I understood why he was so tired during the day.

He had a night life!

Even before I saw the flickering blue light, I could smell the heated plastic of a television waft through the cool dark night. Tienda Soliz had the only television set in our village. We are so high up in these mountains that this television can only get one channel. And that one channel only shows old American westerns.

Pipiolo walked right up to the front of the television and plopped down. The mayor of our village, El Presidente, greeted him nonchalantly.

It was obvious Pipiolo was a regular.

My dog has been watching TV every night! I thought as I hid behind a corner to watch Pipiolo—and the movie, too.

The actor, Juan Wayne, was trapped on the roof of a burning building. Just when it looked as though all was lost, four horses pulling a hay wagon galloped through the town, and as it passed by, Juan Wayne jumped down into the hay to safety. At that moment, Pipiolo jumped up and let out an earthshaking howl. The men in the *tienda* sprang to their feet, visibly shaken. "Get that dog out of here!" shouted El Presidente.

Pipiolo raced out into the street, and I ran after him.

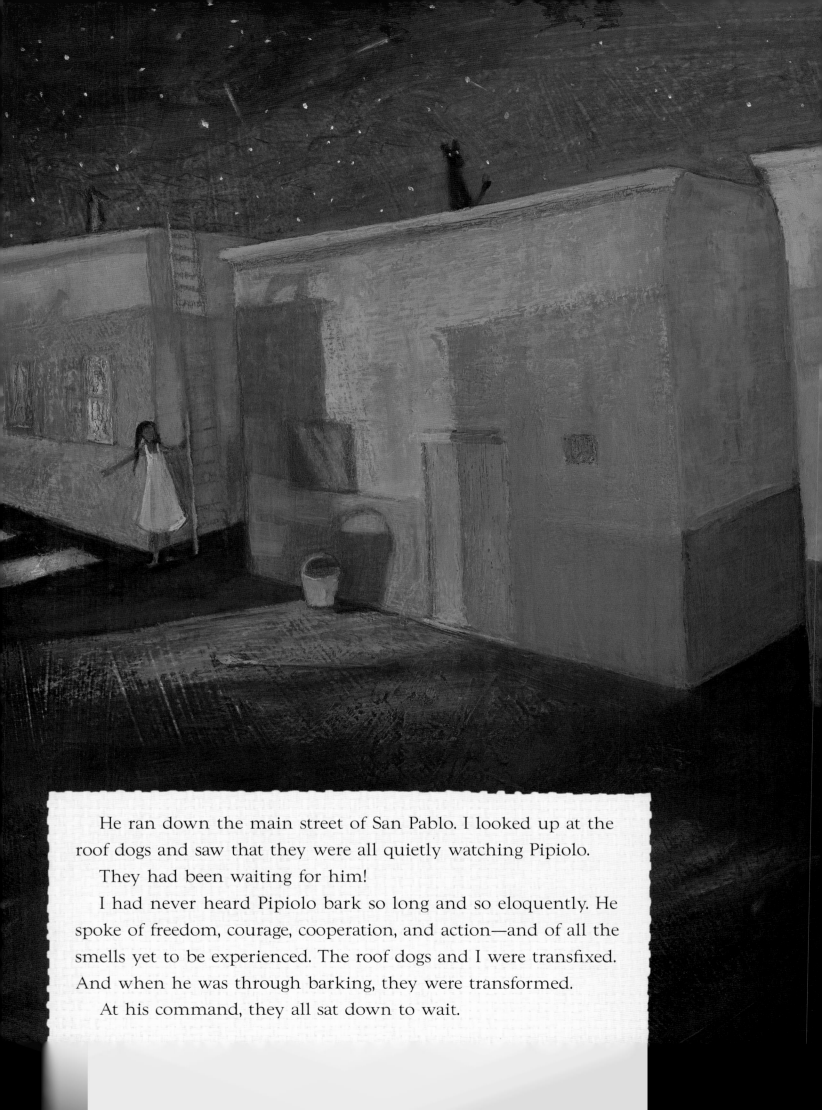

He ran down the main street of San Pablo. I looked up at the roof dogs and saw that they were all quietly watching Pipiolo.

They had been waiting for him!

I had never heard Pipiolo bark so long and so eloquently. He spoke of freedom, courage, cooperation, and action—and of all the smells yet to be experienced. The roof dogs and I were transfixed. And when he was through barking, they were transformed.

At his command, they all sat down to wait.

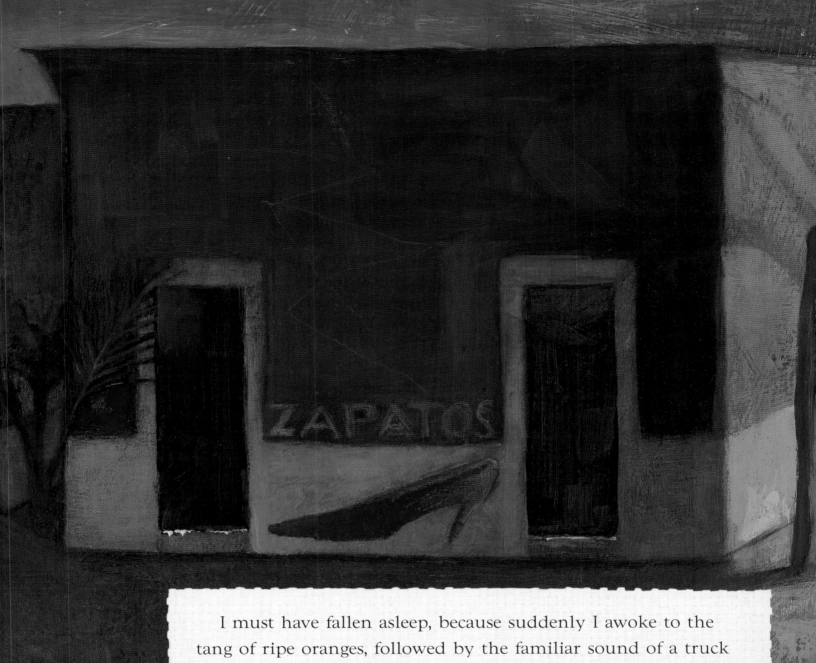

I must have fallen asleep, because suddenly I awoke to the tang of ripe oranges, followed by the familiar sound of a truck grinding its gears as it climbed the long, steep road to our village.

Pipiolo barked, and the roof dogs stood up and began to leap from house to house toward the last two roofs at the end of the village. All, that is, except for Chulita, who shivered, frozen with terror.

The truck stopped at Tienda Soliz to make the delivery of oranges, then drove on to the end of the village to turn around. Pipiolo barked again, and the dogs all jumped down onto the pile of oranges in the back of the truck.

Chulita was now the only dog left. She barked forlornly as the truck started to make its way back through the village—and to leave Chulita behind.

The only roof dog in San Pablo Etla.

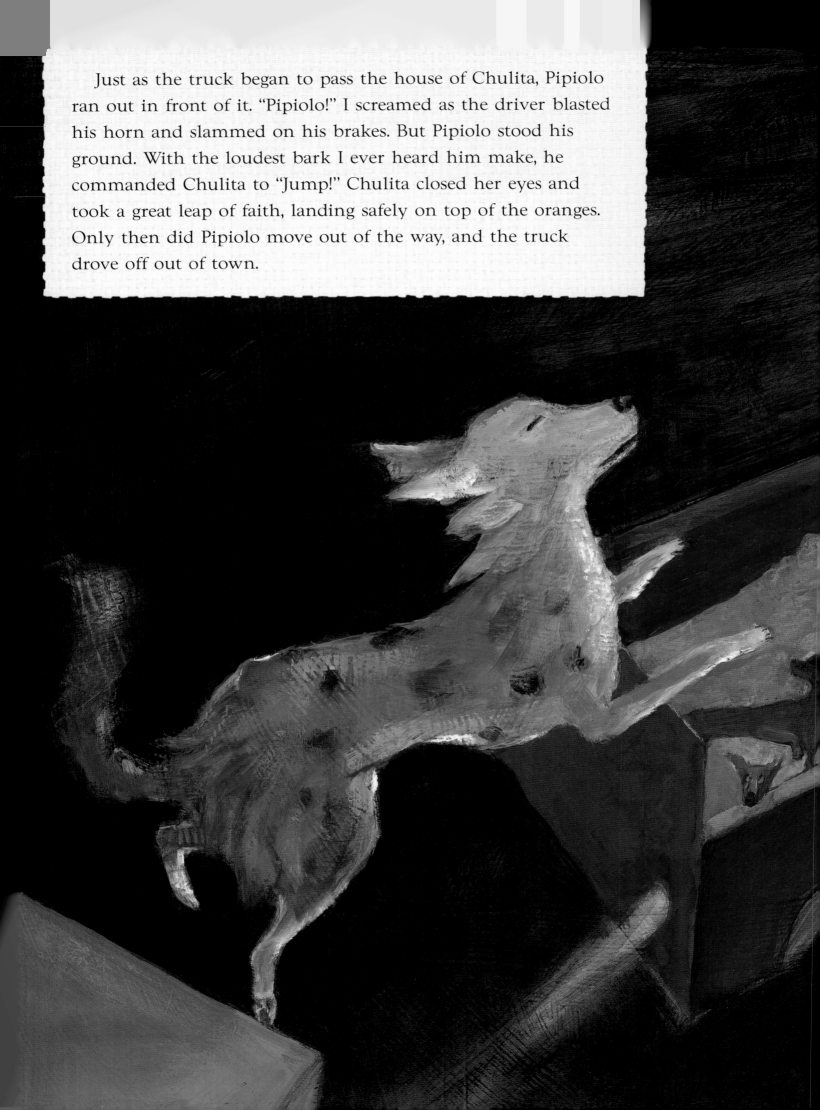

Just as the truck began to pass the house of Chulita, Pipiolo ran out in front of it. "Pipiolo!" I screamed as the driver blasted his horn and slammed on his brakes. But Pipiolo stood his ground. With the loudest bark I ever heard him make, he commanded Chulita to "Jump!" Chulita closed her eyes and took a great leap of faith, landing safely on top of the oranges. Only then did Pipiolo move out of the way, and the truck drove off out of town.

Just before the truck disappeared down the road, I saw all the dogs, one by one, leap off the back of it and follow Pipiolo into the cornfield and out of sight.

As they did, I whispered, "*Tierra y Libertad*—Land and Freedom."

I slowly walked home and crawled into bed. Closing my eyes, I could smell the roof dogs racing through the fields, exhilarated by the first touch of soft earth beneath their paws, their fur moistened by the tall grass. They were headed for the mountains.

As I listened, I heard the joyous barking of the newly free. And in that sound, the voice of one dog stood out among them all. My Pipiolo!

In my small village, things remain the same from day to day. The mysterious disappearance of the roof dogs was the biggest event to ever happen in San Pablo Etla. El Presidente called an emergency meeting and even canceled school. Everyone had a theory, but most agreed that it had to have been some kind of supernatural event. My little cousin, Inocencia, stood up and pronounced it *"El Milagro de San Pablo!"*—the Miracle of San Pablo!

The next morning, I got up especially early to take the long route to school, through the neighboring village of Viquera.

When I stepped out into my yard, I saw Pipiolo curled up in his usual spot under my window! I ran over to give him a big hug, but he was so deeply asleep, I decided not to wake him. Instead, I softly whispered in his ear, "Sleep, my dear Pipiolo. You've been busy, but you have much more to do."

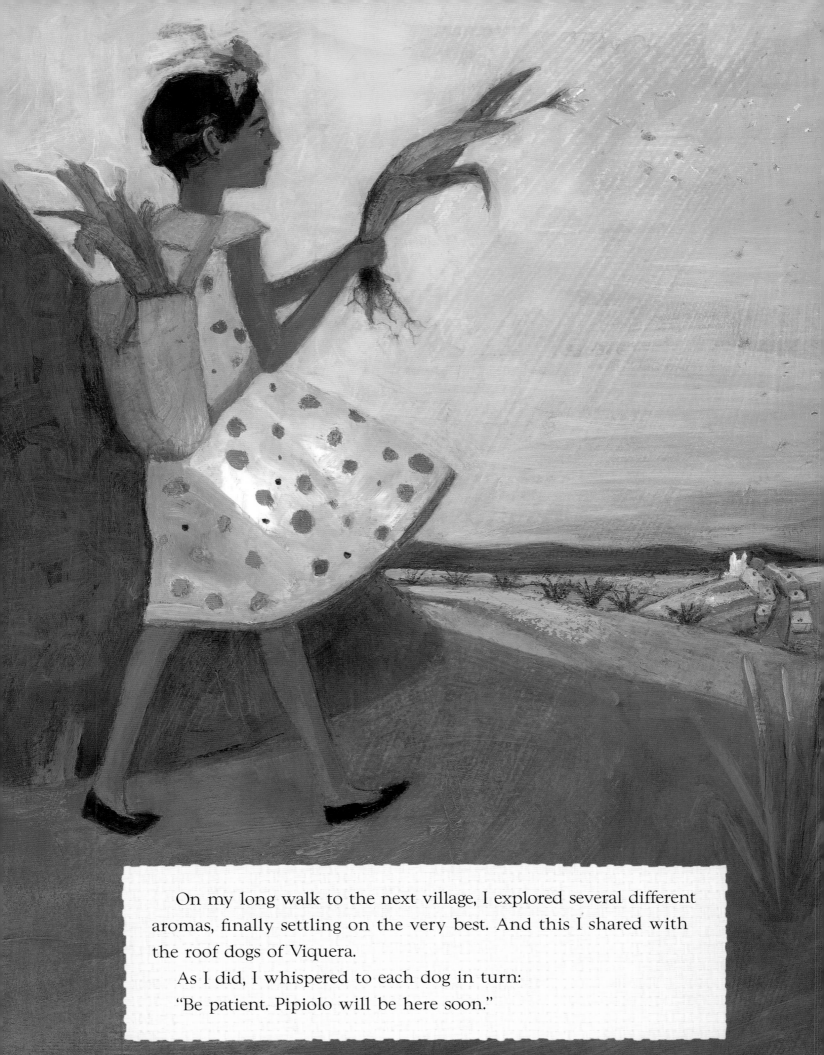

On my long walk to the next village, I explored several different aromas, finally settling on the very best. And this I shared with the roof dogs of Viquera.

As I did, I whispered to each dog in turn:

"Be patient. Pipiolo will be here soon."